WOMAN,
EAT
ME
WHOLE

WOMAN, EAT ME WHOLE

poems

AMA ASANTEWA DIAKA

ecco

An Imprint of HarperCollinsPublishers

HarperCollins books may be purchased for educational, business, or sales promotional use. For information, please email the Special Markets Department at SPsales@harpercollins.com.

Ecco® and HarperCollins® are trademarks of HarperCollins Publishers.

A hardcover edition of this book was published in 2022 by Ecco, an imprint of HarperCollins Publishers.

FIRST ECCO PAPERBACK EDITION PUBLISHED 2023

Designed by Angela Boutin

Library of Congress Cataloging-in-Publication Data has been applied for.

ISBN 978-0-06-309292-1 (pbk.)

23 24 25 26 27 LBC 5 4 3 2 1

*For my mother & all women like the mother of the boy
with five loaves and two fishes: never mentioned, rarely
thought of, but we all know that if she hadn't packed lunch,
the miracle of the 5,000 would've never happened.*

CONTENTS

Woman

Ama Nkrumah

Act 1; Scene 1
Enter woman:

we do not know what she looked like—
how stretched her flesh was laid out in the husk of her being,
how charred her eyes may have been,
how clickety her laughter may have sounded
the elasticity of the jiggle in her behind when her feet
 landed on ground.
We do not know which tribe she came from, who her mother
 was
what language she may have spoken and which name she bore.
we only know that, if there was a palette of colors she would have
 fallen
anywhere between the darkest shade of black to the palest
 hue of brown.
we only know that she was woman.

woman at a political rally.
who claimed space on a soapbox, renamed herself
 in show of solidarity,
slashed her cheeks with blade, smeared blood over her body
and dared all the men present to follow suit to demonstrate that
their collective freedom was worthy of skin-deep sacrifice.
Ama Nkrumah.
a name that did not belong to her.
a voluntary erasure, but an erasure nonetheless,

for what's a name to freedom?
what's breaking of skin to claiming of self?
what's spilling of blood to a wholesome bond?
what's a chance of being shamed to a people saved?

you haven't been loved well enough until you've been loved
  like a man.
Christ didn't come in the body of a woman because even he
  knew he wouldn't have lasted all 33 years with a mouth so holy
  and a tongue that sharp.
when love stretched wide it was only to make space for the
  redemption of men.
when love starved it was only because she dreamt of fed mouths.
when love bled handfuls of pain it damn sure was because there
  was no escaping it.
when love offered dangling breasts at the temple of protests it
  was only because she believed in a kinder tomorrow hard
  enough to be shamed for it.
when love choked on apologies it was only because peace
  was the greater offering.

you haven't been loved well enough until you've been loved
  like a man

Scene rolling on a never-ending roll

SHOOT

(After an altercation with a tutor, Design Academy Eindhoven graduate Yi-Fei Chen created a brass tear gun that fires water collected as tears, as a visual metaphor for her personal struggle with speaking her mind.)

A design student created a brass gun that fires tears she's collected in three stages

1. The user first puts on a mask with a silicone cup that catches the tears.

*MASKS-ON-DISPLAY
:Fake smile 2.1
:Broken but makeup game strong
:Facsimile of generational pain
:Hiding in plain sight
:Mouth stuffed with merry-go-round pain
:Hand-me-down stress
:The atom of a scream
:The square root of a fresh wound
:Neo-spiritual songs

2. The tears are frozen in a bottle.

*SHELVED-FEELINGS
:Pickled anxiety
:Silence heavily spiced with an atrophied tongue
:Ingrown rage
:Skins—burnt umber-cocoa brown-desert sand-charcoal black-

leather jacket black-midnight black
:Body-type—not photoshopped enough
:A collection of *I'm fines* in response to a million *how are yous*
:Less suspicious-looking heartache

3. Which is then loaded into the gun—allowing the frozen tears
   to be fired.

*TEARS
:Angry black woman
:Too loud for a woman
:Diary of a mad woman
:A hashtag movement
:A voice that sounds like someone left a *fuck you* in your throat
:The lifecycle of a scream
:Tears, plain old tears

What does it say of a country
if its women need tear guns before they can cry?

Still woman?

What if I woke up in a different body next Monday?
without a uterus, but still a woman
No longer a hemorrhaging warehouse for eggs

What if I woke up in a different body
next Thursday of the coming week?
A well-soaped nut sack
cushioning a reasonably sized penis,
an innate entitlement for the world's offerings
and pre-installed knowledge
of having inhabited a feminine body?

What if I woke up as the phantom pregnancy
of a woman who'd miscarried?
Living a life of pretense unknown only to me
Bloating and bleeding and puking
my way through a revolution
Will I be woman still?

Will I be woman still, with my outliers forming new identities?
Calling into existence other forms of living
and toe-tagging it to the body of womanhood?
Will I be woman still, leaving a litany of unpardonable mistakes,
forcibly paraded as the masthead for unreal women
Will I be woman still?

Woman

Woman (n): Pleasure valve

Woman (n): Manufacturing plant for babies

Woman (n): Involuntary carrier of a country in her womb

Woman (n): Armed fuselage

Woman (n): God with a big g

Woman (v): Malfunctioning clock

Woman (n): Borderless country

Woman (n): Ungovernable land

Woman (n): Third world country

Woman (adj): god with a small g

Woman (n): Developing country

Woman (v): A sea squirt eating its own brain

Woman (adj): Man's leverage

Woman (n): Poorly paid demanding job

God is a woman

This morning I told God I no longer wanted a uterus,
Could He take it & replace with breasts that fit into a D cup?
I tire of fighting alone
Israel only ever won against Amalek
because Aaron and Hur held Moses' hands up.
My arms grow heavy from doing it all by myself.

Someone I love teaches me how to fight back and still stay safe
   with pepper spray
Someone I admire tweets how he wishes feminism disappeared
He's tired of the different connotations.
I don't know which comes first,
the sound of my heart breaking or my fist clenching.

I'm 19 all over again and telling mother about the boy next door
who kneels under the window to watch me bathe.
Mother's words become a hot slap that resets his entitlement,
and the neighbor across the street is telling her boys
   will always be boys.
And I'm writing about how
Truly, God ought to be a woman

A man tells me he loves women,
Tells me his love for women isn't wedged in feminism.
How do you tailor women to your wants and call it love?
He tells me, write all the poetry you want

God remains a man

a new God then
a God whose hands work after all this dragging
A God who, from constant rejection, births hope

Alien eggs

someone once described peas
as alien eggs
but that snapshot
should be reserved for ovaries

ovaries hold pain hostage
in the bodies of women
ovaries enroll pain in school,
train it until it has a first-class upper degree
in applied ache insensitivity
then gets a well-paying job with a top company
that values it so much
dedicates a set number of days to
making sure women practice
how to not bite their tongues off
how to keep their backs straight
even when their insides burn like kerosene fire

ORDINARY SPEAK

MRN: 0182115-114053-AM

DOB: 27 YRS

SEX: FEMALE

<u>Clinical History</u>: menstrual pain so severe the patient's body bends in half; time twirls in slow motion, becomes one with her womb and dilates to forever. Pain has been a tenant in this body for a long while.

<u>Technique</u>: Squirted gel massaged on abdominal area with a cold iron-like device to evaluate abdomen and pelvis

<u>Findings</u>:
ABDOMINAL USG
Something that aint supposed to grow here, lives here.
Who was it that carried anguish against the ancestors for not resisting colonization?
This body too coils at its own betrayal - as it houses an expat invasion

Liver: all good bruh
Gall bladder: never been better
Kidneys: king of norm
Pancreas and **spleen**: healthy and clean

PELVIC USG
Right ovary: not looking so good love.
Left ovary: just okay for now.

Uterus looking mad shady I aint gonna lie, but so far, all good.

<u>Impression</u>:
1. Findings suggestive of a body trying to eat itself up. Cells spiraling in excess, frothing at the edge of its own mouth, only to swallow it back.
2. Something tied the ovary up in knots. And then, asked it to dance in clots.

V for Pink

They called me Pink
Pink as marrow in the bone of my lineage
safely tucked away so you can't see
but goddamn that shit tastes good.
Hey John Doe, you ever suck marrow?
Ever had juice trickling down your elbow
beg your tongue to slosh it up?
You ever touch your finger to your tongue,
point to the ground and chant walahi I can die happy?
Pink
Pink like how your taste buds spat rebellion
before your tongue knew to control its speech
Pink the way your grandmother's stubbornness (in absentia)
  gave you trauma
Did you know that if you stand two feet away from diluted blood
  it looks pink?
Chewy spongy stretchy bubble me up and down pink
Layers upon layers upon layers of pink
I ain't gotta announce my presence pink
Oh my god this hurts
Oh my god this feels so good
Oh my god, am I not your child too?
Pink

V for Pink (remix)

You ever touch your finger to your tongue,
point to the ground and chant walahi I can die happy?
    Layers upon
    layers upon
    layers of pink
Pink the way your grandmother's stubbornness gave you trauma
Oh my god this hurts

Marrow safely tucked away so you can't see
but goddamn that shit tastes good.
    Chewy spongy stretchy
    bubble me up and down
    pink
I ain't gotta announce my presence pink
Pink as marrow in the bone of my lineage
Oh my god this feels so good

Pink like how your taste buds spat rebellion
before your tongue knew to control its speech
    Hey John Doe,
    you ever
    suck marrow?
Did you know that if you stand two feet away from diluted blood
  it looks pink?
Ever had juice trickling down your elbow
beg your tongue to slosh it up?

Oh my god, am I not your child too?

And they called me Pink
     Pink
      Pink

@mAnsPlainA

@mAnsPlainA: I urge every woman to have a pap smear. Pap smears don't hurt, they may be uncomfortable but they don't hurt

| Tweets | Tweets & replies | Media | Likes |

what is not yours is not yours 🔒 · 10m ⌄
Unbuckle
kick off
unlatch
unhook
strip bare - knee down,
  till there's just skin to slip out

💬 2   ↻   ♡   ⬆   ili

what is not yours is not yours 🔒 · 9m ⌄
Bend knees
Inch forward - a little bit more
Just a little bit more
Hook your feet into the metallic pedal
I'm about to insert the speculum. You'll feel my touch

💬 2   ↻   ♡   ⬆   ili

what is not yours is not yours 🔒 · 4m ⌄
Tense muscles
Fff–
Clenched teeth
Cold. Cold. Cold.
IS THIS THING STILL INSIDE ME??

Jesus! But also Jesus Christ!

💬   ↻   ♡   ⬆

Question

You're going to hate me for this
Oversimplifying your life in another man's tongue
Baring your bottom in public
Whispering loudly about your sponginess as if silence were
  not an option
Poets have no dignity

But haven't I tried to show you, the underpants
you clutch to so desperately,   leaks from your open gates?
You bawled yourself to sleep in this place
                                  bled in this place
died and resurrected a watered-down version of yourself in this place
Stymied desires that aren't dead and buried yet in this place
Yet you wait for nirvana
to transform grief disguised as love
                              into a shade that complements your skin

Your mother taught you how to howl to ward off shadows
Your father made you a nonbeliever of conventional love
Together
   they have made a being whose war cry trembles the earth
But in the face of it, war cries don't stop bullets
You dent your knees in prayer
for a request God keeps far away from you
I am tired of watching you bleed from the same old gash
I am burnt out from seeing you dig into your wounds
Who taught you that scratching a wound speeds its healing?

Reminder

A love recipe hangs down my mother's neck
She loves without a manual
Muscle memory syncs her heart with her mind
and makes her a metaphor for softness
When pain blurs love
I look at her and remember to breathe

Missed opportunity

With scream and spittle
The pastor at the front seat of the trotro condemns women
For sitting in church with hands clasped fervently
As if they didn't bleed out a baby two weeks ago

When the passengers utter a feeble amen to his halleluyah
He tells them they can do better
than offer God sick Amens.

I smile in pity
He's missed countless opportunities to meet God,
because he's been too busy condemning her
in exchange for cedi notes

Start: restart

Bodies should function like video games
Round one: score some points
fatal jab, ominous music, you lose.
Round two: lights dim, new game, new body

Instead we're stuck in pods
That bruise, scar, wound,
Clot, bleed and fall apart
Bodies that do everything but become new

Brains should function like apps
Updates fixing features that don't work—
Upgrades that enhance the entire system
Brains that loop bad memories
and sound an alarm when incompatible material comes in contact—
not after it's penetrated and touched base with our selves.

Bodies should function like video game characters
Start, score, lose,
Restart

A Good Day for Redemption

Dear Nalorm,

Now that we both agree our twenties are home to ruin, our bodies have become liberation grounds for redemption. The late-night calls, the salt-laced shots, the outrageous twenty-cedi taxi fare for a ten-minute journey after 1am, the tipsy laughter, the pitiful ritual of guilt-tripping old lovers by disappearing, whole man-parts drilled into our black holes in search of missing orgasms. We've both been pretending we've seen the light at the end of the goddamn awful tunnel. But we were so eager to claim this adulthood title we forgot we hadn't grown up. Truth be told, if I could have the cockiness with which naivete knew your body's address and rented space there in your adolescence, I would snatch it. The freedom that comes with not knowing enough about the cruelty of the world to remember to be ashamed of your body. The short length of time it takes to get ready to step out because you're not pinching or poking or burrowing like your skin is target practice for greenhorns. An old lover once told me he was sitting on an undiscovered gold mine because he was dating a flat-chested girl who he hoped would become voluptuous in the future. And my face lit up because I believed myself an undiscovered gold mine. You can blame everything on youth if you're drunk enough; his illegal touch, food spiced with low self-esteem, a body that doesn't know how to forgive itself. Nalorm, my high school dormitory was built on an old cemetery. The way I see it, either we're feeding off the dead, or dead things were laid here to rest so we could live each day new. The Old Testament God promised joy in the

morning, but there's no way of telling time in dark tunnels.
So any day is a good day for redemption.

Love,
your older self

The audacity of men

Days after a stranger
kisses your lips without permission
You struggle to give language to the way you feel
Filth doesn't feel very far from the surface
It lingers like a dead rat taking forever to decompose
And guilt lives underneath
But trapped guilt is like mercury,
it will slip through the tiniest crack
And you carry it quietly,
waiting for an opportunity to trash it
Because how else do you make sense
of a random unknown man
Whose muscle memory dares entertain the thought
of touching a woman without her consent?
How else?

False teachings

There are lectures
on how to dress
like a respectable woman
How to show less skin
How to stay put when night falls
How to not breathe too damn hard lest you excite loins

There are no lectures on how to respect a woman
regardless of what she wears
How to exercise self-control
or what consent means
This land would rather teach its daughters how not to get hurt
than teach its sons how not to hurt

Love Yourself

Chip.
    Chip.
Chip.
Chisel approximately 3.5 inches of flesh out of the waist area
Lift the breast to a firm position until it is perky and a perfect D cup
Add three layers of skin until the backside can vibrate with a single
  poke
Tone the leg muscles until men can see their reflection in your
  gleaming skin
Widen the hip until it is the exact curve of a bass clef
Chip.
    Chip.
Chip
Perfect your body until it is a cross between a writer's
description of the girl a woman's husband leaves her for
and a photoshop guru's final masterpiece
Soften your muscles, don't be too boyish
You don't want to have kids? There must be a glitch
You cannot be too skinny
You cannot be too f a t
You cannot be team itty-bitty
You can't have boobs that s a g
You cannot have a small ass, what's there to hold?
You cannot love your body until somebody says so
You can only love your stretch marks

when they are a map for a man to find your tucked away treasure

Pit women against each other let's find out who's fresher
Tell women they're the queens and

then go right ahead and be the crowns.
Checkmate, there goes the clown
You cannot want to have it all
You cannot want to follow just one path
You cannot have too much makeup
You have to look natural but not the kind of natural

that makes you look like you just woke up from a 36-hour sleep
Everything you do is a free license for critique
You are to swallow your pride like it doesn't have a sour aftertaste
You are to be a perfect balance; not too acid, not too alkaline
You are to be a conscientious being who

meanders perfectly between soft and hard
You are to be a funky Friday night

mixed with a tinge of Monday seriousness

and a hint of Sunday calm
You are to be all the colors

of the rainbow at the same damn time
Everything you do

is an open invitation for condemnation
So love yourself anyway
Love the brown and the bounce out of your skin

Love the unholiness of your lips
Love the 9am happy face stitched on
Love the ugly feet and the awkward teeth
Love the high-pitched laughter that grinds everybody's gears
Love the intricacies of your mind and how it keeps you up all night
Love the parts of you you're waiting for someone else to love

before you learn to love yourself wholly

Everything you do is an open invitation for condemnation,
so go ahead and love yourself anyway

Girl to Woman

I wonder when you stop feeling like a girl and start feeling like
   a woman.
When your mind finally agrees with your body that you're in fact
   nowhere near twenty-one.
When woman doesn't feel like a skin you're waiting to fit into.
When you do not forget to address your own self as woman.
Does it wake you up with a persistent ache like period pain?
Does it dawn on you while sitting at the back of an Uber you took
   for some sense of safety?
Does it throb within your entire body when you learn to l e a v e
   and call **even that**—love?
Does it silently mock you like old favorite clothes that suddenly no
   longer know how to climb your body?
Or does it propel you into comfort the way a bra coming off does?
When an aunt at a cousin's wedding tells you to hurry up and marry
   because even the neighbors in her neighborhood are asking when
   you will marry,
You know she will give your mother grief for months but the hot air
   that prances around your ears when you tell her you wish both she
   and her neighbors long life because the wait may be a long one.
—is that precisely the moment you become woman?

Mathematician

You've always been good at math
From the one plus ones to the $3x^2 - 2xy + c$
To 3 times the square root of four divided by 5 times 9 equals
   10.8 and nothing less
To Pythagorean theorem tangents
You've always been good at math
So you knew that good grades + firm hands +
a patient heart raised to the power three,
equaled the start of a great nursing career
And good looks + great hips multiplied by excellent cooking,
a healthy dose of attraction, lots of ambition,
with a common denominator of relentless love equaled a great
   marriage
And great genes, great timing, 3 ounces of good loving
and a little bit of skill equaled a beautiful son.
And when his first word was mama, your heart did a thump thump
   sound
your mind will later learn to calculate
And when he learned how to walk on his own without your hands
   to guide his tiny little feet,
you sucked your teeth because that was an equation solved right
And when his grade was a metaphor for excellence,
you were not surprised because you wrote that expression
And when he was ten and he told you he was going to be an engineer,
you smiled because tick tock, tick tock—
it was all coming together;
You have always been good at math.

When he's 14, there's a new tik, but not on your watch.

It's not part of the equation. Nobody ever fits sentences into
  quantum theory.

But you don't lose your balance because blood doesn't burn easy

And when addiction lives so comfortably in his body that you
  no longer recognize

the boy you made with your own body, you do not stumble

And when you are forced to build bars to shut your own baby out,

you tell yourself you're drowning and you must teach yourself
  how to swim

before your lungs collapse

And when you wrestle a knife out of his hands,

you wonder if you will get this equation right.

Your heart is breaking, and you can't pray it away,

you can't beg it away, you can't work it away,

you can't starve it away, you can't drive it away,

you can't threaten it away. You can't even therapy it away

And so you strangle it.

The very life you pushed out.

You tug and pull and squeeze, until there is no more heart to break

And you wonder to yourself,

if you were ever really good at this thing called math

(Ellen Pakkies, a Lavender Hill mother whose 20-year-old son, Abie, exemplified
the zombified, kleptomaniac "tik monsters" that prowl the streets of Lavender Hill,
had tried everything she could think of to get him off the addictive tik. But after
more than six years of living hell, she decided she could take no more. On a cold
morning in September 2007 she tied a rope around Abie's neck and strangled him
to death.)

Sum

Some days,

I am a

sum

of all the women

I failed to save

That-which-must-not-be-named

- /fem•i•nist/—urban dictionary: a woman who seems to think that her ability to push a baby out of her vagina entitles her to bigger and better everything

- feminist! /You've got to say it/and put your back into it/—the word first popped up in the nineteenth century and has now been transformed into a term of abuse aimed at young women who show the slightest hint of superiority.

- Feminist—synonym for rebellion

- Feminist—for women, by women, about women

- feminist—a remarkably effective word for inciting the discomfort of someone who believes in equal rights and opportunities, practices it like a devout Christian that attends church on Sundays and weekdays. But wants absolutely nothing to do with the word feminist. Retweets a tweet about feminism that doesn't have *feminism* in it.

- Feminist: the smallest unit of the female anatomy

- feminist—most likely an ugly, bitter and unmarried woman who hasn't had good dick in days, and who should probably be punished with no dick if she insists on arguing rudely about equality for women in capital letters on the interwebs.

- FEMINIST—an insurgent more dedicated than a Jehovah's Witness. Committed to preaching the gospel of women as God-ordained equals of men, and not dependents or playthings. Occasionally creates Twitter threads calling men out in English too complex for them to understand, much less give a fuck about.

- ~~feminist~~—no! the right term should be egalitarian, one who believes in *true equality* for all, not that bullshit feminazism.

- feminist: well-educated, petty bourgeoisie with a malice and vindictiveness towards men, who can afford daily taxi rides and thinks fast-food joints that don't have enough branches are a travesty.

- feminist—one who thinks the world should work in a way that is reflective of how women struggle with balancing their career, marriage, kids, identity politics and the rest . . . espouses all the feminist ideals but explicitly states that she's in fact NOT a feminist. Shies away like it's Ebola, vehemently supports how unfeminist she is by stating how she will never pay for dinner.

- Feminist: a less obvious way for men to get into the pants of young women.

- feminist: a tyrannical fanatic who crushes anybody who steps out of *the* line. A little like the mainstream artists whose wack songs go viral, overshadowing the countless dope underground ones.

- Feminist: a glass of diluted apple cider vinegar

- feminist: a footnote of national politics

- /fem•i•nist/—Merriam-Webster definition: someone who believes that men and women should have equal rights and opportunities

When they ask if you're a feminist,   will your hand shoot up?
will you be a supporting act or a qualifier for the cause?
will you be a prop for the main show,
or a question mark when the curtains rise?

will you be mere spice garnishing the main dish?
or the main course that's too bland, or too much, or not enough?
will you be a sophisticated dessert that makes an appearance
on the menu according to the size of our purse?
will you be sucked in or gurgled or whispered or spat out?

When they ask if you're a feminist,   will your hand stay up?

Eat

Take, Eat

I have left parts of myself on your son's body
I whispered my name around his beautiful hollow navel
Spent quality time inside his mouth
Kneaded my tongue against his
tasted him
Tasted desire in the way his muscles lie
prostrate when my lips touch his
Sexual attraction only lasts 6 weeks
It's been two years since we kissed:
Does the sign of the cross
Hands clasped.
Whispers amen
It's time to eat.

Woman = pain

Smile too hard, be fat, show skin,
fully clothed, be "ripe for plucking"
Young pretty black thing,
own a vagina, own a womb,
breasts that bounce, hard flat chests,
At the post office, in the bedroom, with an uncle,
beside a lover, in a safe space, in a strange land
Whether you toggle it between mild or extreme, or just being:
Woman = pain
With throats forced open to swallow loss
Loss so wide it swallows our body into a kind of silence
Trauma tendrils its way into our flesh
In our waking hours,
our brain wears nothing
but the memory of an aching body
There's no closure
There's no release
There's only god at the hollow of our pain

Our utopias are different

You think my struggle is a privilege.
You think insensitive landladies,
a business on wobbling knees
and a body that struggles to stay alive
is a vague recollection of a dream you will never have.
I think your polished floors and your rent-free house
and not having to worry about food
is a bus my mother missed
the day before she met and fell in love
with my father

You want to be the kind of person
whose suffering has a name people can identify with
I want to be the kind of person who doesn't suffer
The longing in my body nears its expiration date
When it dies I shall be birthed with a new longing
The longing in your body has been on the shelf for far too long
How fucked up is it that your utopia is my hell

And my utopia is the reality you want to escape from
Look how we're both scarred with the terrible impulse to keep
  wanting
Look how we bleed from all this wanting

Uses

He used "I love you"
as compensation
for all the ways
he failed to love her
She used "I love you"
as an antidote
to pause the rot

my love is a warm pot of soup

It took me minutes to write that down
I knew I had to get this right
I don't want to be a plagiarized poem shining through
  a glorious mimicking light
Try so hard to impress and lose the crown before the fight
I want to love you so hard that you would be programmed
  inside of my being
When I was a little girl my eyebrows were just one monobrow
But fashion, growth, teenage laughter and wanting to fit in
  split it into two
And every couple of months the hairs reach for each other
  and try to become one again
And you and I, we are just like that
We make confessionals out of mouths
and heal ourselves back to wholeness when we break
and I don't want to be corny and say we will be symphonies
  of a great melody,
but the bassline in *bodies* is so distractingly beautiful
that we cannot be anything but that

my love will make you smile from unspoken fulfilled expectations
and parts of you will start singing halleluyah even before
the sermon starts

Me

god in every nook

pain twists your body into the shape of a wounded heron
the doctor uses a cartoon face from 0 to 10 as a scale
the pain crescendos inside your shoulder
not skin deep, not bone bruise—
inside. deep within. a place your fingers can't reach
if you could just dig your fingers and caress, perhaps the pain
  will subside
pain surging like a charged wave, spitting out of its own mouth
  froth of excess
as though a demon calls its name
    and then,
in a moment of indecisiveness
it shrinks back into a slow beat
only to resume after a while
you want to say the pain is one that blinds you so slowly
you can see the gene of the orange wall—
a crisp sweltering color that glides into your brain to supersede its
  numbness.
Is this how white noise feels?

you want to say pain so stale it surprises you such mold can thrive
you want to say 11. but you point to 10 on the chart and grind your
    teeth

This place where you are right now*

anxiety crochets your belly into a bad fit
when your account hits negative for the sixteenth time

This place where you are right now
God circled on a map for you

at night, a dream of your almost-mother-in-law
starts as prayer and ends in an unsent message
you wake, booger tearing eyelids apart
survive this, survive anything

This place where you are right now

the thing about hunger is that it knows how to rage
and how to fade into a calm quiet
    when you remember how much food
you would be eating if you were in your mother's house,
it roars

This place where you are right now
God circled on a map for you
Our Beloved has bowed there knowing

how shitty your lovers feel:
to them the way you articulate your hurt
matters

more than actual wounds they've carved into you
this astounds you

This place where you are right now
God circled on a map for you
Our Beloved has bowed there knowing
You were coming.

Feet, wander to where gloom flees.

*"this place where you are right now" by Hafiz

the awesome in Me

I want to loan God all my insecurities
Ugly and heavy as they are
But it's hard
The other day I called myself an insufferable prick
for not being able to sit through a social gathering
without feeling like I was suffocating
Last month I didn't think it necessary to celebrate a great win
I bury my wins under a heap of nonchalance
Because inadequacy grows here and never dies
I am harder on myself than anyone will ever be
I am harder on myself than I will ever be on anyone
Irritation pops up like a "terms of service" button
that refuses to activate until I've read through all the conditions
Guilt pins me down for not being the best version of myself yet
I forget to celebrate the little joys,
I forget to celebrate the parts of me that bring others joy
So when people call me amazing, I double-check to make sure it's me
And look around for a mirror, to see if I can spot the awesome
  in me too

Transmogrified dreamer and a God with a Wi-Fi connection

I wake up needing to forgive myself even harder.
I want to crawl back to the mouth of my pain and snatch myself back.

Did I not ask you, God?

I thought my love could thaw the apathy away.

How dare me call this love a violence.

racking up points

I swallowed up all the red flags and
now they've become wounds that won't stop bleeding.

I want to crawl back to the mouth of my pain and snatch myself back

You have dreams

Some are bigger than your country's debt
Some are ticking nonstop like a throbbing ache
Some are jerking your muscles the way torn ligaments do.
Occasionally, you chant them as a peace offering to self-love
And try to convince yourself
that delay doesn't equate to redundancy.
You refuse to indulge in regrets
So you bring your dreams to your chest,
and hug them
When time is done wounding your heels,
you will emerge a better sportsman.

New·roses

/neu-ro-sis/

I worry about privilege
And what it will do to my unborn children
I want insulated roofs
and plates King Midas need not touch.
A mind that's at ease
and wealth that will pad my great-granddaughter's seat
even before her father is formed in the womb.

I worry about the immunity it bestows
and the bloody outcome
children stuck with a comfortable world's eye view
or worse, placing their empathy
in leather purses
when it should be bumping fists with their sensibilities

I worry about how forthcoming I will be with my staggering love
if the knowledge of it will cripple their intelligence
It heightens my anxiety knowing that wealth
can be a substitute for all shades of blind
I'm uneasy about this Black Card birthright
That can envelop my babies and slather them in a womb of apathy

Even before they get here

Jigsaw

I wonder
if my parents
know the shape of my trauma

I want to call my mother in the dead of night
and tell her 1 Corinthians 13: 4–8 is a love
that only exists in the pages of worn-out Bibles

I wonder if my father knows the peak of this body's betrayal
How my pain—the exposed nerve of a broken tooth
Hyperlinks to my swaying emotions

How temper spumes at the jaw of this body
High as the gates of Israel
Torrential, like its wars

How I love men who want me to shrink
And each time
How I want them to stay

I wonder
if my parents
even know that I have trauma

If they know it keeps morphing
Into jigsaws that press
into old wounds to create new ones

that I have become
a resilient body waking to new dawns
testament to a war no one sees me fighting

Loose faith

I once loved a man with hands so soft
he could touch feelings into existence
He tried to make a safe space out of my body
when I hadn't found comfort in my own skin yet
He lost his sensitive vocabulary inside a heartbreak
so he comes off as misogynistic
And being so chained to this
I couldn't pull away for shit
And so I lost my faith underneath my own tongue

Anatomy of a body

there is genius residing in your pores
this body has survived you loving it only on some days
this body has survived being the place you go to sin
this body has survived a hurricane named after all your mistakes

this body has:
stunned you into stillness each time it remolded your skin
taught you how to shape the lonely at the end of a heartbreak
                      into something more governable
tipped over your goodness into your folds as cache for
returning to your self
glowed you up when loss shrunk you in

there is genius residing in your pores
gods bow down at your feet
say a prayer before they eat
and ask for more

Mirror, mirror

There are days when the gravity
of all that needs mending in my life—
presses down on my larynx
sits a heavy tumor in my belly
gnaws at my reasoning like a crisis.
    Days when I have run out of faces to keep up appearances
    I feel like an ellipsis. Waiting for the good to come
    When the inner self goes down on its knees asking for life to
       come to a halt
Then I remember that I am the very personification of God
Face molded like an artist with a unique style and endless edits
Voice so velvety it could be FDA approved

Brain wired to keep rewiring itself towards redemption
A body that has taught itself how to hold on to life the way pain
  holds on to women
    And when the mirror smiles back at me for seeing another day
      to its end
    I'm reminded of why self-love will never go out of fashion
    Because life is fucking hard
    But my God, aren't we god?

Let it be

I have been fretting over things that God shakes his head at
Toying with faith as if it were a disappearing act;
One minute I'm full of it,
The next, I don't exactly know the shape of it
I fret over now and tomorrow
Giving myself and God a headache.
Spoon-feed myself faith,
And come up hungry again.
I have taken up all the space on my mother's prayer sheet
And the happiness of those I love takes up all of mine.
At the end of day we're both in God's ears
Saying let it be

Our Father who art in heaven

1 Sometime in November she talks
about how sometime in June she runs
out of things to say. Her throat became a
cave that could no longer spit words out.
Cascading hangers transmit grief through
touching shoulders. Silence begets space
begets nonchalance begets stiffness begets pain.

2 Emotions so loud it must make some kind of bad singing
Relationship as an unripe pawpaw: naive, firm, promising,
mellowed, pukey yellow, so-so, lax, browning, rotting.
Everybody wants to pause the rot for divergent whys.

3 And this too will be prayer
Asking for rage to sit longer in your chest
so loss has no room to stymie your righteousness
This too will be prayer. Won't it?

4 The blood stain on your brother's singlet
after the accident looked like a seven.
That's how precisely you remember her telling you
that you have the luxury of tangible pain to justify your sadness.
As if agony were cotton candy we display on sunny parks to see:

5 Whose is biggest
Whose burn is acute
Whose color bleeds downwards

Whose can be put on hold so another can be magnified

6 And this too will be prayer
Asking God to gift her with all the pain she can wear as clothes,
visible and glaring, so she no longer feels guilty for her intangible
  sorrow
And feverishly mumbling *father forgive me*
Equal parts anger, equal parts repentance
This too will be prayer. Won't it?

Building blocks

.On the
morning
of the
sixth day,
I save a
seat for
you,
again.
We
giggle
and
analyze
and pass
notes
about
babysitting
which you
will have no
recollection
of

.On the
evening of
the eighth
day, you
climb into
my bed
and I
rewatch
*Orange
Is the New
Black* with
you just
so I can
understand
your
delightful
pockets
of laughter

.Before
we
leave,
we
hug
and I
know
I'm
going
to love
you
forever

.You
must be
tired of
how often
I tell you I
hope he
hits his
big toe
against a
sofa, but
you let
me vent
anyway

.It feels
like
you've
been here
forever,
alarm
bells go
off when
we've not
heard
from each
other all
day

.You
bleed,
I bleed.
We try
unsucces
sfully to
suture
each
other up

.All
things
come
to an
end
don't
they?

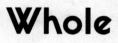
Whole

Saltwater

When teeth bite tongue,
Saltwater diffuses pain
Here, teeth will be what is known
Here, tongue will be what should have been named
Here, saltwater will be our saving grace

When a tongue shrinks on its own do you swallow it whole
  or stretch it out?

Here is the story of a stretch of land before it is named Ghana
Here is the history of a country thousands of years before
  the 18th century
Land that lives on the pages of an alternative universe
A universe the most gifted of world builders haven't dared imagine

A world whose mechanisms science cannot account for
An alternative realm nonconvergent with the future

In this universe, there are
Men with 3D-printed hair,
bristle and coal-black, an aboi so sharp it could make a well-
  constructed road
Men with eyes like a deep scoop of honey
skin different shades of sun setting
voice like the relief you feel
after holding in pee for too long
Men with glinting muscles that compete with sun rays

They grew this land
Stretched it whole
Fought for this land when white people sprouted
And on the 19th of every moon
Young men of the land,
Assisted by the gray-haired
so as not to spray directionless shot wads
of silky potent semen onto fertile ground
After four and a half months of elders watering and talking
  sweet nothings,
Little baby boys would bloom
And grow to continue the cycle of fighting
for what's rightfully theirs
until their turn to make babies
This is the history of a land before it became Ghana

When a tongue shrinks on its own do you swallow it whole
  or stretch it out?

Surely, this has to be why no woman is named
in the history of the country
up until the rise of Yaa Asantewaa
It must have been that the concept of a woman was fathomless
Because no woman was significant in the becoming of this country
No woman toiled and bled and ruled to make this country what it is
No woman was deemed worthy to be named

It has to be, that an alternative universe existed before 18th century
A universe filled with men stale, crunchy, blown up, shriveled
Men industrious, logical, foolish, grounded
Men rich, poor, pretty, ugly, resourceful,
The home keepers, the cooks, the farmers, the child bearers, the
  warriors, the kingmakers
Men who birthed resilience from the innards of a land made gold
Men who made this country what it is.

When a tongue shrinks on its own do you swallow it whole
  or stretch it out?

Men named our women into nonexistence
All this biting into flesh
All this blood
Where is our saltwater?

Formation

I belong	to Accra
A city	named after ants
Who	built a kingdom overlapping generations,
buried	their wounds into the ground,
and	made way for humans to dwell on it

on the	9th of May 2001,
127	people lost their lives
in a	stampede at the Accra Sports Stadium
They	died under the feet of others
in a	formation of rows,
five to	six bodies per row.
To	overcome obstacles and survive harsh environments

fire ants	link their bodies together
to form	an assemblage of escape
you	would think a people dwelling in the city of ants
would	learn their ways of survival
soft-	spoken, fully covered, eyes lowered, pious and polite—
definition	of a feminine body that can thrive safely in Accra
chatty	—strip
half	bosom—strip
above	the knee—strip
childless	—strip
unmarried	—strip
Strip.	Strip. Strip
Until it	fits the mold of what their women ought to be

We live on their land
But we are not like the ants

Bloom

I could write about how bodies are the most malleable things
I could fill a page with how pain leaves words hanging in your throat
I could write a poem about the way people soften up
when their lovers kiss the small of their back
I tried to write something musical about my city and I did not
   know where to start
When I walk through south of Labadi, the streets are bursting with
   an abundance of heritage;
I can tell from the way the dark-skinned woman with the y-shaped
   scar on her left leg
scrubs her baby, that she is a woman who believes in redemption.

Two boys are moving like they've got too much rhythm in their
  bodies
and not enough time to dance it out
A little girl sucks on a lollipop, spits in her hand and offers it
to her small sister, who gleefully licks it up
They have a look on their face that tells that they know
what they're doing is ridiculous and sweet and terrible;
they know wrong isn't right, but they do it anyway
On the pavement, a porridge seller is giving out smiles
like they are Amens to needy requests

A man is telling a stranger that he doesn't even like porridge,
but the way she throws her head back when she drinks it down,
does things to him.
And her laughter tumbles down like the hollow echo of a djembe
What he doesn't know is that this is her first laugh in days.
Old Ms. Atta has a tight-lipped smile as if
her mouth is holding on to sins yet to be forgotten
And when she sings akwaaba ɔdɔ, she means it.
These people teach me,
that if you are from Accra and you are placed anywhere in the world,
there's no way you won't know how to bloom

A utopia for black girls

here, home is a rippling effect of joy in continuum.
which is to say that there is no need for safe spaces
because everywhere is safe.
the spring in our step is directly proportional to the elasticity of joy.
our footsteps are fertilizer for bloom because we walk freely:
in neighborhoods, our own compounds, in the parking lot,
at the grocery store, in a friend's bedroom, at a night club,
in broad daylight, underneath a bridge, in the classroom,
unknown places, late late at night.
fear is a strange phenomenon we keep hearing of—
trying to descend in a spaceship on our land.
but as far as we know? shit don't exist.
safety is communion bread that takes its time to melt underneath
    our tongues

here, neither Rachel nor Leah need to go through the needle
of male validation to attain worthiness.
when the gavel hits wood we are not found guilty of love
our love is not shoved down our throats as mutilated parts of our
    own bodies
it is not sliced up like beef and cramped into an airtight container
to be buried in a man's backyard.
it is not beaten blue until our skins become playground
for primary colors to play mix and match.
memory isn't a trigger that belts grief on you.
love does not return back to us empty or broken.
it does not misfire our brains and turn our emotions into rot.

it does not transform our bodies into a putrid scent of trauma.
here, the loss of our lives does not stink on us while we are still alive.

our births are weights that hold secured futures firmly in place.
our names are melodies so gossamer you can carry them
  in your throat.
our black skins siphon wealth for several tomorrows.
our labor yields fruit a thousandfold.
there are so many smiles per minute we stitch them into billboards
for wandering strangers to soak in for free.
our brown bodies—a climaxing spring.
bodies dancing wild in sweaty arenas with an abandon
that closely resembles unbridled giggle.
how wide the soul stretches when the body has freedom to move!
what is breaking loose to a free spirit?

here, we sing and teach and fly birds into factories,
spinning silk for our shimmery skins.
we sculpt empathy and code the future
and cook healing into hemlines as hedges for our hefty hips.
we build engines and design tomorrow
and palm poems as portals for possibilities.
here, we're eating light
and it tastes like the childlike simplicity
of never even knowing of worry to be wary of it.

Saturday Evening WhatsApp Message

In the last week of August, Andrew Stoecklein—a Californian
    pastor—killed himself.
He turned 30 last May. He was married with two kids, had been
    having some health complications (he'd had two surgeries to
    remove a mass from his chest) and was suffering from
    depression and anxiety.
I keep going back to read articles about him/his death.
Is suicide a sin? I know some countries criminalize it but is it a sin?
Does Andrew still have a shot at heaven now that he's killed himself?
Often I think I'd like the path of Christianity to be like the
    highest degree you can obtain in a field of study.
Once you get a PhD you become an expert—
    yes you don't ever stop learning but you're learned enough
    to never not sink.
Instead faith is a thing we have to summon anew every hour.

When I write poems about dying and pain for my poetry
    workshop class,
they critique the poem like they do every other—
    skin to bone, lines that work,
how to make it read better, "the word sadness appears at least
    5 times can some of it be substituted for another?"
They make my poem better. But they don't make me better.
The thing about repetition is that it lends itself to normalcy.
And that's not such a bad thing if it's ordinary.
But if after years, you still have the same pain,
it becomes part of your identity to the people who

know you, but for you,
the pain is always always new.

Sometimes, I cry so hard I can feel it in my ribs.
I feel like the real me is backed into a corner inside me
astounded by how deep this other me's sorrow is.
I want to be resilient forever. I am happy when I overcome.
Sometimes I think that one day I will break open and write the
  boneless truth.
But I have learned that nobody truly knows what to do about pain.
So I choke my sorrow down and slip my happy face on.

Letter to Afua

Afua, if it weren't for God and you, one day they would find me dead in my studio apartment and finally discover that I do not wear panties.

I hope you laughed, if this were my final letter I would like to know that I left still cackling at things of this world.

During Lent's 40 days, Christians refrain from saying halleluyah, they refrain from rejoicing—from giving God praise. Instead, they remember rot & pain & the senselessness of dead and dying things. They lament until after the 40th day. They bury their halleluyahs.

Some days my body looks wrong on me. I awake with a fist breathing beyond my skin. As though someone angered my insides while I went to sleep, and revenge has to be had.

When will this body finish burying its halleluyahs?

I think often of how the equanimity of Ghana hugely relies on the temperament of the people. As if by some stroke of some bizarre fortune, a genetic migration bundled us all up—which is why we know relative peace, and not because the laws of the land are largely functional.

Everybody is rattled by Ahmed Hussein-Suale's killing, it's not so much that we deem ourselves invincible, but that a targeted killing happened here in Accra. Accra? Ghana?

It reminds me of a random conversation during lunch, where I learn from a friend that the reason why the human body, which is made up of up to 60% water, doesn't leak out (or in) is only because the skin cell has a 14-sided shape that forms an effective barrier.

And for a moment I think we are taking our orientation, our

"Ghanianess," for granted, but I look at the news again, and see that our Ghanianess ain't shit after all.

w-i-p

The city is known for looking like a work in progress;
For making therapists out of passengers for taxi drivers
For protesting and dismissing issues
in the time it takes for a baby to take a nap,
For telling fortunes and sending warning messages
disguised as public signs on the back of public transport:
God is good,
dzi wo fie asem,
no where cool,
nipa yɛ bad,
for sale,
dabi dabi ɛbɛyɛ yie.

Masked Commoners

We become art in an attempt to skip the death chair
We become poets in an attempt to skip shrink sessions
We become rappers in an attempt to transform
our manifestos into a way of being
We become nuanced in an attempt to get the bigger picture.

We tether our humanity to doing good for looking good's sake
One man's sorrow is another man's headline
To become a blowout success from another man's tragedy
Be your brother's keeper becomes feed off your brother's pain
We're rewriting the Scriptures in blood, we are Judas Iscariot
  all over again
We juxtapose our monsters with our inner children
and expect the purity of that inner child to triumph over our own evil,
but we forget that sometimes, children are monsters too.

We're so fixated on balancing ourselves on the line between
  epic and tragic
that "I'm fine" becomes a motto
"I'm fine"—said in a drawl so automated you can taste the unbelief
wafting off the tips of our tongues
We tie the love for our country to a chair and torture it with politics
We starve it and bribe it
Teach it tricks and parade it as party politics
We hang love by a noose and suffocate it
We torture it with variations of "it's not you, it's me" talk
With "when I said I loved you in April,

in that moment, no word has ever been truer" but in October
"baby I don't think we can be"
As if love was represented by smoke,
moving through spaces, never settling.

In the end, we're all ordinary people in disguise.

Acknowledgments

Grateful to the spaces that have nurtured both my stubbornness and my writing: Ehalakasa, FEMRITE, Farafina Trust Creative Workshop and the family I gained from it, and the poetry community in Accra.

Thank you to my teachers at SAIC, especially Janet Desaulniers, and my course mates, for their insight, tenderness and critiques.

Immensely grateful to Daniel Halpern, for believing in this book as much as I do. And to the team at Ecco, especially Gabriella Doob, for the attentiveness and patience.

A huge thank-you to my agent, Rena Rossner; when I take stock of my miracles, I include you.

Thank you to the editors of *New-Generation African Poets: A Chapbook Box Set (Sita)*, where three of the poems in this book first appeared.

And finally, dearest reader, thank you!